Auctioned to the Mountain Man

Highest Bidder

Hope Ford

Auctioned to the Mountain Man © 2023 by Hope Ford

Editor: Kasi Alexander

Proofreader: Nicole Graf

Cover Design: Cormar Covers

MAGGIE

"Don't be mad."

I clench my eyes and blow out a breath just trying to imagine what it is this time. Any time Elana, my best friend and boss, says those three words, I know I'm probably going to end up mad. The first time she said it to me, I laughed it off. We were in our final year of college, and I had just met her the week prior. She had planned a party in our dorm and invited the whole Alpha Theta fraternity. It wouldn't have been so bad if I didn't have a big exam the next morning at seven a.m.

I force a smile to my face. "Is this worse than the time I had to stay in the library all night to avoid the Alpha Theta party and almost failed my exam because I was exhausted?"

She shakes her head, but before I let her say anything, I continue, "Okay, is this worse than the time we broke down in Jasper, and instead of calling your brothers to come get us, you thought it was fine to hitchhike back to campus?"

She puts her hand on her hip. "Trust me, riding with a hitchhiker was a better idea than calling either of my brothers. They would have flipped out if they knew I was—"

I interrupt her with a nod of my head. "Right. At the sex club. So is this worse than the time when you told me that we were going to a book club meeting at the library in the city but instead you took me to the sex club?"

She is completely unfazed as she looks at her freshly painted nails. "You said you wanted to lose your virginity. I was trying to help you out."

I stalk toward her and whisper loudly, "Really! Why don't you say that a little louder? I'm sure the men setting up tables over there didn't hear you."

Elana laughs and flips her hair, unbothered. "Just say it, Mags! You would live a boring life if it wasn't for me."

Begrudgingly, I shrug. There's some truth in what she's saying. I have always been the responsible one. I studied, got good grades, and did what I was supposed to do. Since I met Elana, life has definitely gotten more interesting. "Okay, I give up. What are you telling me not to be mad about?"

She crosses her arms over her chest and juts her chin out at me. "Are you going to be mad?"

I mirror her actions and smirk at her. "Probably. What did you do?"

She gives me her best smile. "I got us dates for tonight."

I throw my hands up. "Nope. No way. I'm working. This is a work event. It's the biggest fundraiser of the year, and I need to be able to concentrate on what's happening. I can't be entertaining some guy I don't even know. Nope. It's not happening."

I turn away from her and go back to arranging the centerpiece on the table. Tonight is Moonshine Mountain Distillery's annual fundraiser. It happens every year, but this will be the first year I'm attending. I know how important this is to the family, and I've done everything I can to make sure everything goes off without a hitch. Plus, with the new social media campaign I started, there are more high rollers planning to attend than ever before, which in turn means more money will be donated to the local hospital.

There's no way I'm going to get caught up in one of Elana's schemes.

I can feel her staring a hole in my back. "Forget it, Elana. I'm not doing it."

She comes to stand beside me and grabs my arm. "Will you stop? The centerpiece looked perfect ten minutes ago. Look around this room; everything is perfect. You're freaking out for nothing."

I cross my arms on my chest and challenge her. "That's easy for you to say. You're part owner. You graduated college and instantly became director of public relations—"

She scrunches her nose up, and I hold my hand out. "Let me finish. You deserve the position, and everyone knows it. The point I'm making is you've trained for this job since you were little. College for you was just something to bide your time until you were able to take over your position. You don't have to prove anything to anyone. I, on the other hand, got this job because you are my best friend. I do have something to prove, and bringing a date to a work function is not a smart thing for me to do."

She rolls her eyes and laughs. "It'll be fine."

Exasperated, I pull away from her and move to the next table to get it set up. "Fine? Fine like the time you set me up on a blind date, and it ended up being my psychology professor?"

She giggles. "He was hot."

"Oh my God, Elana, he thought I set the whole thing up. I swear for the rest of the semester, he thought I was stalking him."

She points at me. "You got an A, though."

My voice rises with indignation. "I always got A's."

"See? No harm, no foul."

I shake my head but can't hold back my laugh. This has to be why Elana and I get along so well. We are complete opposites in every way, but she livens up every situation. "Tonight is important to me, Elana. They are calling this the party of the year. That's huge, and if everything goes off without a hitch, we can raise a lot of money for the pediatric hospital."

"I know how important tonight is, Maggie."

As soon as I hear the dip in Elana's voice, I want to kick myself. "Elana... I'm sorry. Of course you know how important tonight is. I wasn't thinking."

She busies herself working on the centerpiece at the table next to where I'm standing. "It's fine. Yes, this fundraiser is important. When our parents died, my brothers and I wanted to do something in their memory, and the pediatric hospital that my mom worked at would be what they want. They've been gone for a long time, Mags. I'm fine."

I move over to stand next to her. "I know you're fine. You're one of the strongest women I know, Elana. And I really do know how important tonight is to you. Your parents would be so proud of you."

She takes a deep breath and nods her head. "I know." She smiles at me. "Did I tell you? My brother is coming tonight too. He promised."

I squeeze her arm and move to the next table. "The elusive Bentley? I'll be honest with you, I can't wait to meet him." Elana and her two brothers are owners of Moonshine Mountain Distillery. Their dad started the company years ago, and when their parents passed, the three of them inherited it. The oldest, Edward, is acting manager, and I see him every day. Bentley is the one that I've never met and everyone is hush hush about. I can't even get the scoop from Elana about him.

Elana threads her arm through mine. "You'll get to meet him. He won't stay long. Crowds are not his thing, so he'll be in and out, but he'll want to meet you. He's heard all about your social media plans for the company."

I try to keep my mouth shut, but I can't. "It's just so weird. I see Edward every day, but I don't even know what Bentley looks like. No one talks about him, and he's never at the board meetings or anything. I mean, it's obvious you love him and think highly of him, but he's like a mystery man. What's his deal?"

She shrugs, and I see the indecision on her face. She gets like this any time we're talking about her brother. "Bentley is... look, he's a great guy."

I burst out with a laugh. "Really? You don't sound very convincing."

She swats me on the shoulder. "He is. He would do anything for me, and I know if I ever needed him, he would be there for me. He's just been through some stuff..."

It's obvious she's uncomfortable with this, and that's not what I want. I know Elana, and I know that even though she acts like it's not a big deal, tonight is important, and it's going to be hard for her. I don't need to interrogate her about her brother anymore, especially since I'm going to get to meet him in a few hours. "Okay, so back to work. What's left to do?"

She pulls out her phone and starts swiping. "Tables, check. Centerpieces, check. The audio and visual team has set up, and everything is ready. The itinerary of speeches for tonight are scheduled, and everyone's received copies so they know where to be and when. There's only one thing left that needs done."

I breathe out a sigh of relief. One thing. I can handle one more thing. I feel like I've been working double-time for so long it's nice to know that after tonight I'm going to have a little bit of a breather. "Okay. What's left?"

"Get ourselves ready for the party."

She starts pulling me toward the door, and I go willingly. "About the date—" I start.

She huffs as she pushes the button on the elevator that will take us upstairs to the corporate offices. "It's not a big deal. Tom and Cole know we have to work tonight too. They'll enjoy dinner, and I told them to bring their checkbooks. If nothing else, you can have a drink with Cole to see if you do want to go on a date with him."

I want to argue with her, but I don't. It would be pointless anyway. Elana always gets her way, and knowing what tonight is and how much it means to her, I'm not going to fight her on it. "A drink. I can fit him in for a drink, but seriously, I want to make sure that tonight goes off without a hitch, so that's it."

She jumps up and down excitedly, and I grab her to stop her. "One drink, Elana. This is not a date."

With a big smile and eyes lit up in mischief, she

nods. "A drink... I got it. We are going to have so much fun tonight, Mags. I just feel like something big is going to happen."

I shake my head as we get onto the elevator because I know Elana, and most likely she's right. If it's up to her, something big will happen tonight. I just don't know if I'm ready for it.

BEN

I pull at the collar of my shirt and then rotate my shoulders. Everything about tonight is uncomfortable. The dress pants, the buttoned-up shirt, the too-tight jacket that constricts every movement I try to make, and the mass of people that are milling around. I've been to this event every year for the last four years, and I've never seen a turnout like this one.

I make my way through the crowd, and my skin crawls because I can feel all eyes are on me. No doubt they are either wondering what the missing brother is doing here or they're trying to figure out who the bearded mystery man is that obviously doesn't fit in. I do my best to ignore it all and make my way to the bar. I'm sure that we have supplied the alcohol for tonight, and it's tempting to order an Old Fashioned made with our Moonshine bourbon, but I plan on driving out of here tonight, and I know if I have one drink, my sister Elana will use that as an excuse to take my keys and try to keep me here. No thank you.

"What can I get you?" the bartender asks me.

"Just a water, please."

His eyebrows lift in surprise, but he nods as he puts the glass under the spout and fills it. "Thanks," I tell him as I gulp it down. I hate having my back to the crowd, but this is the best way to keep conversation limited.

I look at my watch and am counting down the time until I get to leave. I promised my sister I'd come, but as soon as I make an appearance and talk to Elana, I will be leaving.

I hear my brother before I see him. "Well, well, well. He does come off the mountain. What's up, little brother?"

I grit my jaw and turn in my seat. I may be his younger brother, but I'm at least four inches taller and have a good thirty pounds on him. I stand up, wanting to tower over him. "What's up, 'little' brother?"

He laughs, causing me to do the same. I don't resist when he reaches for me, and I wrap him up in a bear hug, lifting him off his feet.

When I set him on the ground, he's straightening

his hair and then his tie. "Thanks for coming, Ben. It's all Elana's been talking about."

I nod and sit back down in the chair. "Sure. I don't think I can stay long but... I'm here." I blow out a breath and clench my hands together to stop myself from pulling at my collar or removing my jacket altogether.

Edward crosses his arms over his chest. "So you can't stay long? Something pressing up on the mountain you just have to get back to?"

I almost look at my watch. On the way here, I was thinking about how long it would be before Edward gave me shit about not coming off the mountain. Unable to resist, I glance at the time. "I've been here exactly four minutes, Edward. I think that's a record for you busting my balls."

He laughs heartily. "Some things never change, brother."

I roll my eyes and stick my thumb over my shoulder. "Can I get you a drink?"

He comes to sit next to me. "Nope. I am planning to stay sober—until after my speech, at least. That is, unless you'd like to do the talking this year. I don't mind at all."

I sit with my arms over my chest and my back ramrod straight. "No thanks. Not interested."

Edward shrugs. I'm sure he felt he had to give it a shot, but at least it doesn't appear he had his hopes up that I'd be filling in for him or anything. "Admit it, you love this kind of thing."

I gesture around the room, but my brother doesn't look anywhere but at me. The only indication he's listening to me is the slight tilt of his head. He opens his mouth and closes it again.

It's tempting to walk out of here, but there's a part of me that feels guilty, as if I've deserted my brother and sister to handle everything while I hide out on the mountain. "Spit it out. Go ahead and get it off your chest. I can handle it."

He leans back as if this is just a random conversation, but I know my big brother. He's planned this conversation out and probably even practiced it in the mirror. I don't rush him. I sit quietly and watch him, waiting for him to say what's on his mind.

He rubs his hand across his clean-shaven jaw. "Look, I know we all have our strengths. We each serve the company in different ways."

"Fuck, Eddie. I know I'm not pulling my weight."

He slides to the edge of his seat. "Yes you are, man. That's not what I'm saying, just hear me out. The truth is you hiding out on that mountain has turned into the best possible scenario for the business. The research you've done on stills and every-thing you do on the actual production is amazing. Would I rather have you down here helping me with the legal, accounting, public relations part of it? Hell, yeah! But I know you're best suited where you're at."

I'm not understanding. "Oookay... so what's the problem then?"

He puts one hand on my shoulder and squeezes. "If you were happy up on that mountain, doing your thing, it would be one thing. But you're not. You're up there stewing, letting the past eat you alive—"

I interrupt him. "I'm not going to talk about this here."

He releases me, and his shoulders slump. "Fine. All I'm saying is forget the guilt. Your contribution to the business hasn't gone unnoticed, and you are exactly where we need you to be."

He wants to say more, and I hold my breath waiting for it. When he doesn't continue, I nod my head. "Got it, man. And I appreciate it. I love being up on the mountain. I really do. But yeah, there's shit I need to work through. I'll uh, do better."

His eyes pop out of his head. I know that's prob-ably the last thing he expected me to say. I've never admitted that I have a problem, and maybe this is the very first step on this long journey of getting over my shit.

I stand up and stuff my hands into my jacket pockets. "All right, enough bullshit. You have a speech to give, and I need some air."

I jerk my head toward one of the back entrances, and Edward nods his head. "If I don't see you later, thanks for coming, and I'll see you tomorrow at our weekly meeting to do a recap of tonight."

I nod and almost get away before he stops me. "And Ben, just because you are on a video call, it is a business meeting."

His nose is scrunched up, and he shakes his head. "Wear a damn shirt."

I laugh. I probably shouldn't because he's right, but yeah, I laugh. "Sure thing, big brother. Shirt. Got it."

I wave bye to him and make my way through the people laughing, drinking, and talking. When you're by yourself 99 percent of the time, events like this are a little overwhelming. Just a quick breath of air, then I'll find Elana, and then I'll get to head back up my mountain.

MAGGIE

Everything is ready.

I've driven myself batty. I've double- and triple-checked everything until there's nothing left for me to do. I've paced around the party, made sure everyone knows where they're supposed to be and when, and I've talked until I'm all peopled out. I had to escape, and even though I should feel guilty about it, I don't.

I lean back on the swing, slowly rocking back and forth. The only light here in the courtyard are the tiki lights that have been set up and the light from the flames in the stone fireplace.

I lean my head back and look up at the starry sky. *I did it.*

The sense of accomplishment I feel is like nothing

I've felt before. It just proves that doing this, the social media, the planning and coordinating, is exactly what I should be doing. I love my job, and I can't screw it up.

A door opens, and I hear the noise from inside before it shuts again. I tense in my seat, hoping it's not Elana with our "dates."

Curiosity gets the better of me, and I turn in my seat. The man walking toward me hasn't spotted me yet, and I suck in a breath as I look at his broad shoulders, long beard, and dark hair that is longer than most. I've never seen him before. I tried to read up on everyone that I knew would be in attendance tonight, and I definitely don't recall him. Could he be the "date" that Elana has set me up on? My hopes go up for all of two seconds before I squash them. No way that is him. Elana is always trying to set me up, and it's usually with men that are too put-together, a little snooty, and definitely wouldn't be caught with facial hair. Not that length, anyway.

"Hey," I call out in the semi darkness so I don't spook him.

He doesn't jump or even slow down. His head turns, and when his eyes find me, I'm wondering if maybe he did know I was here the whole time. "Hey. Sorry to interrupt you, but I needed a breather."

His voice is deep and raspy. It's almost like he

doesn't use it often. I shrug and turn back in my seat. I have to in order to force myself to stop staring at him. "Me too."

He stops next to me and crosses his arms over his chest. "You don't like crowds?"

I shrug, with my eyes on the fire. "They don't usually bother me, but it's been a crazy day. I just wanted to soak all this in for a minute."

He looks around. "This is nice out here."

I nod. "It really is. It's even better during the day. The view of Moonshine Mountain is like nothing you've ever seen before. I would literally sit out here all day if I could."

"So you've been here before."

I hold back my smile. "A few times." I look at him standing awkwardly beside me. There are other chairs surrounding the fire, but the swing is by far the best seat and the closest to the fire. I put my toe down to stop the slow movements. "You want to sit down?"

His eyes round, but he nods his head. He grumbles as he takes off his jacket and throws it on the back of a chair before settling next to me. He slowly starts to rock back and forth, and I watch as he rolls his sleeves up. His forearms are thick and corded, and I watch his muscles flex as he moves to the other arm. Both arms are covered in ink, but I can't make it out in the semi-darkness.

I barely resist waving my hand in front of my face to cool off. Dang, who is this guy? It's on the tip of my tongue to ask him when he turns in his seat and faces me, putting his arm along the back of the swing. "So you like the mountains?"

I point toward the space out in front of us. "I love those mountains. I mean, I'm sure you've seen them. They're beautiful."

He pulls at his collar. "Do you go there much? Hiking or anything?"

I shake my head. "No, I'm not much of a hiker."

"You—"

"What—"

We both start at the same time, and I laugh. "You go ahead."

"No way. Ladies first."

I turn in my seat as much as I can, but it's impossible to do unless I want to flash him my underwear. I reach for the hem of my skirt and hold it down as I lift one leg on the swing and cross my other leg over it until we're facing each other. "Do I know you? I'm pretty sure I know everyone that was on the list, but I don't remember you."

He eyes me thoughtfully as he strokes his hand

through his beard. "What? Is that your way of saying I don't fit in here?"

My mouth drops, and I can feel the heat rise on my face. "I wasn't saying that at all. Oh my gosh, no. You're perfect... I mean... you could fit in anywhere... I mean... you sort of stand out." I slam my mouth shut and put my hand to my head. "Shut up, Maggie."

I start to mumble through my embarrassment, and he laughs. It's a deep chuckle, and I bring my head up. "Are you laughing at me?"

He nods. "Yeah, you're cute."

I blanch. "Cute? Uh, thanks... I think."

Truth is, he's older than me. That much I can tell. And to him, I'm probably some blubbering kid. "I better get back in there," I tell him, even though I remain in my spot.

"Are you the party planner?"

I shrug. "Something like that."

He tilts his head to the side and looks at me. "What's that look?"

What do I tell him? I can't say that I'm attracted to him and thought we were maybe getting to know each other and I'm a little disappointed because obviously he thinks I'm a "cute" kid. Heck, he probably thinks I'm here with my parents. No way he'll believe I helped plan this event. He needed a breather, and I just happened to be in the right spot. No. I can't say any of that. Instead, I stall. "What look? You just met me. You don't know if I'm giving a look or not."

His hand comes off the back of the swing, and he brushes my hair off my face and behind my shoulder. I lean toward him and catch myself before I do something stupid.

He's watching me closely, and I can't take my eyes off his. "I may have just met you, but I know your name is Maggie. That's what you just called yourself, anyway. And I saw the shift in you. You seemed happy... almost content. And then I tell you you're cute, and you freeze up on me. Was that too forward?" He holds his hands up, palms facing me. "I can keep my hands to myself."

I almost blow him off and tell him he's imagining things, but where has being safe ever gotten me? Nowhere. I just met him, and most likely, I'll never see him again. "You're right... geez, I don't even know your name."

He hesitates for just a minute. "Ben."

I try to remember the name Ben from the list of people that bought tickets for tonight, and I don't remember anyone. Could he be someone's plus one? I keep my tone light. "Okay, well, Ben, you're right. There was a shift in me. I'm always the cute one." Oh

God, that sounds so conceited. But I force myself to continue. "No one ever sees me as anything more than the 'cute' friend. I mean, just once, I want someone to find me irresistible. That's all. And yeah, we just met, but maybe I was hoping..."

I let my voice trail off. Geez, what is wrong with me? I'm practically begging this man to want me, and I know nothing about him. I unfold my legs and stand up. "I better get back in there. It was nice meeting you, Ben."

I don't want to leave. If anything, I want to stay and listen to his deep voice as he talks about anything and nothing. But I have work to do, and I can't do it from out here. I wave awkwardly at him and turn away with fists clenched at my sides. Walking away from him doesn't feel right, but what choice do I have?

BEN

"Stop," I tell her as I jump up from the swing. "Please, don't go."

She stops, but her back is still to me.

I don't know what I'm doing. She's the first woman that I've been attracted to in what feels like forever, and I don't want to let her walk away. I take the few steps between us and reach for her hand, lacing our fingers together. She's slight compared to me, but somehow our hands fit together perfectly.

"Look at me, Maggie."

She turns around and leans her head back to meet my eyes. "I really should go."

I pull her hand, and she falls against me, her body pressed against mine. "Stay. There's something I should tell you."

Her eyes widen, and her breath hitches. I try to tamp down my arousal, but being this close to her and feeling her body next to mine is proving more than I can handle. How is it that I just met her and I can't let her walk away? "So you didn't like it that I said you are cute?"

She shrugs, and the movement has her hair falling forward, hiding her eyes from me. I brush it off her face and put my hand on her cheek. "I only said you were cute, but the truth is, I think you're beautiful. You're the most beautiful woman I've ever seen."

She leans toward me but doesn't say anything.

"Talk to me, Maggie. Tell me if you want me to walk away."

She shakes her head slowly. "No, I don't. I want..."

She stops, and I hold my breath, waiting for her to finish. She licks her lips and stares at me with wide, innocent eyes. I lean down until our mouths are mere inches from each other. "What do you want? Tell me."

I'm holding her too tightly, but I can't let her go. She goes to her tiptoes, and her voice is soft as a whisper. "I want you to kiss me."

I release her hand and cup her face in my palm, searching her eyes. When I was getting ready for tonight, I was filled with dread and tried to figure out how I could get out of it. Now, all I can do is feel thankful that I'm here because I would have hated to have missed this. I lean down before I can consider all the reasons why kissing her is a bad idea.

As soon as my lips touch hers, I have my arms wrapped around her, holding her flush against me. Every one of my senses are heightened, and I know that I don't want to let her go. I tilt my head to deepen the kiss. She whimpers as she digs her nails into my waist, pulling me closer. My hands slide down her back, and I cup her ass, lifting her up so she can feel my bulge pressed into her belly. She leans into me as her hands slide under my shirt. As soon as her bare fingers graze my waist, I pull back, breathless.

Never in my life have I wanted someone as much as I want her right now. Panting, I tell her, "Go home with me."

Her mouth falls open. "You want me to go home with you?"

I lean my forehead against hers, still trying to get my bearings, and hiss, "Yes. Fuck yes."

She looks unsure, and I put my hands on each side of her neck. "You don't have to."

"I want to, but..."

I tighten my hold on her. "But what?"

She bites her lip and looks almost embarrassed.

"I've never gone home with someone I just met. I don't even know you."

I grab both her hands in mine and lace our fingers together. "We can get to know each other here tonight."

"Okay."

"Okay?" I ask her, making sure I heard her right.

She laughs. "Yes. I need to go in now. At least until after the presentation of the checks. Then, if you still want me to—"

I cut her off. "I'll still want you to."

She takes a deep breath and lets it out in a burst of air. "If you still want me to go home with you... then I'll go."

I pull her with me to grab my jacket that I left on the back of the chair. With our fingers still laced together, I pull her to the door that leads back into the party. I feel like I'm in a rush now, wanting to get this over with so I can get her outta here.

My trepidation from earlier is gone. I walk into the party without any hesitation. My brother is up on the stage, making his presentation. I look around the room for my sister. I have to see her while I'm here, and then as soon as Eddie is done with his speech, I'm taking Maggie out of here.

It's like I can feel the shift in her. One minute she's

looking up at me, a smile on her face. The next minute, she's pulling her hand from mine and looking across the room. I follow her gaze and spot my sister. She's making her way to me as everyone around us starts to clap. The presentation is done, and I can get Maggie out of here... soon.

"You came!" Elana says as she wraps her arms around me.

My voice is gruff, half-filled with frustration. "I told you I would."

She pulls back and slaps me on the chest. "I know, but when I couldn't find you, I'd wondered if you'd bailed on me."

My frown deepens. "I wouldn't do that." I mean, I thought about it, but I didn't do it. I wouldn't do it.

"Oh my gosh, have you met Maggie? Maggie, this is my big brother, Bentley. Ben, this is my best friend and partner in crime, Maggie. She's the one that's doing the social media for us now." I don't know if I could be more shocked. I turn to look at Maggie, and for the first time, I realize exactly how much younger she is than me. She's my little sister's age. Heck, she probably just finished school. I take a step away, putting some distance between Maggie and me. "Hi, Maggie. It's nice to meet you."

My voice doesn't even sound like my own.

Maggie's nose scrunches up, and she looks between my sister and me. She's confused, that much is obvious. "Uh, hi Ben. It's nice to finally meet you."

"Oh my God, Cole! Maggie, this is your date. We've been searching everywhere for you. Cole, Maggie. Maggie, Cole."

I grunt at one of the men that's been standing behind my sister and now walks toward Maggie. He takes her hand in his and leans down to kiss her cheek. It takes everything in me to stay rooted in my spot. I can't hear what he's saying to her, but she keeps looking at me with those big eyes of hers.

I should have gotten her out of here while I could. She's my little sister's best friend, she's an employee—hell, my employee—and she has a date. I let my guard down for all of ten minutes, and in that span of time, I found the one woman I shouldn't want and can't have. Fuck my life.

I clear my throat, and both Maggie and Elana look at me. "I'm going to head out."

Elana reaches for me. "No, you just got here. We haven't gotten to talk at all. You can't leave yet."

I pull my little sister into a hug. "I'm proud of you, sis. Everything was perfect."

Her face softens as she looks up at me. "I wish I could take the credit, but it was all Maggie."

I glance at Maggie, and she's looking at me with hope in her eyes. What was I doing thinking that I could have anything with her? She deserves more than a one-night stand, and that's all I have to give. There are a thousand reasons why I need to walk out of here. I force the words out, and they sound lifeless and professional. "Thank you for everything you've done for the company, Maggie. We appreciate your hard work."

Her eyebrows arch in surprise, but before she gets a word out, Edward joins us. I slap him on the back. "Good job, bro. Now, it's time for me to get out of here. Let me know if you need anything."

I walk away without another glance at Maggie. I can't look at her because I know if I do, I may not be able to walk away.

MAGGIE

Ben walks away without even glancing at me.

I should let him go, but as soon as he disappears out the door, I know I have to go after him.

I turn to Cole. "I'm so sorry. I need to check on something."

Elana tries to stop me, but I tell her I'll be right back. I don't wait for her to respond; instead, I go as fast as I can toward the door that Ben just walked out of.

He's already halfway across the parking lot by the time I catch up with him. Out of breath, I call his name. "Ben."

He stops, and his shoulders rise and then fall as if he just took a big breath. I say his name again. "Ben."

He turns, and the look on his face tells me he's out of patience. What happened? How did he go from the man that was ready to take me home to now he doesn't even want to look at me? "You're just going to leave?"

He crosses his arms over his chest. "That's what I was doing, wasn't I?"

I rear back in surprise. He doesn't even sound like the same man that I talked to—that I kissed—earlier. "I don't understand. What happened back there?"

He lifts his chin, but he doesn't say anything.

"Ben, if you changed your mind, fine. But at least be man enough to say it."

He laughs, and the sound is ominous in the dark parking lot. "You have a lot of nerve, you know that, right?"

My mouth falls open. Is he saying that because I followed him out here? "Why? Because I go after what I want?"

He chuckles. "Oh? You want me? What about what's-his-name?"

I shake my head in confusion. "Who are you talking about?"

He spits out the words. "What was his name? Cole?"

It takes me a moment to figure out who he's

talking about. I point toward the building I just walked out of and then I throw a hand in the air. "What does he have to do with anything?"

"You're here on a date with another man." He spits out the words as if he's disgusted even saying it. Is he jealous? It sure sounds like it, but there's no way that's possible.

"What? I told Elana I wasn't going to go on a date tonight. She'd already invited him, and I told her I would have a drink with him. That's all."

His jaw tightens, and he stares at me with his arms crossed over his expansive chest. "It doesn't matter. You're an employee. You work for me."

My mind shifts to all the times I've been asked out by a coworker and I've told them no because it's against the rules to date within the company. It was always a good excuse for me because I was never attracted to any of the men I work with. But with Ben, I'm willing to break all the rules, and that's not like me at all. "You own the place. I think if you wanted to hook up with someone, you could."

"So a hookup? That's what you want? A good fuckin'?"

I can feel the heat rise on my cheeks, and I'm glad we're outside in the darkened parking lot. He doesn't know the truth about me. He doesn't know that I'm a virgin and have never considered going home with a man before. Not before now... not until him. I'm not going to tell him either because that would be just another excuse of why he can't take me home with him. "So what? Now I'm cheap? Forget it, Ben. Forgive me for thinking there was some kind of connection between the two of us. I didn't realize I was coming off as a desperate slut. Sorry for wasting your time."

I turn on my heel, intent on getting away as fast as I can. I can feel the tears welling in my eyes, and I'm doing my best to hold them in.

"Maggie, wait."

I don't stop, though, and I get to the sidewalk before I feel his hand wrapped around mine, and he jerks me back toward him. I land with a thud against his chest. Instantly, his arms are around me, and he's holding me to him. His cock is hard and pressed into my belly. I shouldn't, I know I shouldn't. I'm pissed at him right now, but it doesn't stop me from lifting my hips, loving the feel of him against me.

"Ben, what are you doing?"

He's panting as his eyes search my face. His eyes are wide and glazed over. "Ben." I say his name, thinking I can bring him out of his trance.

He leans his forehead against mine. His voice is hard, and it seems like each word is being dragged out of him. "For the first time in a long time, I forgot."

I don't want to say anything because I don't want him to let me go. I've never felt this way in a man's arms before. It's as if I belong, and I'm protected. I whisper the words to him. "Forgot what?"

He clenches his eyes shut. "It doesn't matter."

I reach for him, cupping my hand against his cheek. "It matters to me."

He opens his eyes, and they are almost black as he stares back at me. "None of this matters... I thought..." He shakes his head and physically puts me away from him. "I wanted one night, Maggie, and this is getting too complicated."

"Complicated? What's complicated about it? I'm not asking you for anything. I wanted to go home with you. You're the one that bailed on me." Why do I feel like I'm begging him? I hate the pleading sound of my voice, but it just shows how much I want him.

He takes a step back and drops his hands, clenching them into fists at his sides. "You're my employee. You're my little sister's best friend. You're here, on a date, with another man. That's too complicated when all I was wanting was to sink my dick into some hot piece of ass."

I clutch my hand to my chest and rear back as if he actually hit me or something. Did he really just say that? "Fuck you, Bentley."

I run as fast as I can away from him, and he doesn't try to stop me this time. Instead of going in the front door, I walk down the sidewalk to the back entrance. I think I've been humiliated enough. I don't need to walk into the middle of a party with tears streaming down my face.

I push the code into the door to open it and find myself on the back elevator that will take me to my office upstairs. Leaning against the back of it, I try to get myself together. I shouldn't let this bother me as much as it is. I literally just met the man.

But as soon as that thought crosses my mind, I squash it because I've never felt a connection to anyone like I felt with him. I was ready to go home with him. Hell, I was ready to give him my virginity after only knowing him for thirty minutes. Am I that hard up? Or was there really something between us? It seems I'll never know the answer to that. I suck in a deep breath and try to hold back more tears.

The elevator dings, and the door opens. I step out into the empty hallway toward the solitude of my office. I know I'm going to have to make an appearance downstairs, but it's going to have to wait. Right now, I need to pull myself together and do my best to forget about HIM.

BEN

I watch her run from me. She can't seem to get away fast enough since she is fuckin' sprinting in her high heels to get away. After everything I just said to her and seeing the hurt on her face, why do I want to run after her more than anything else right now?

I fucked up.

I know I did, and there's nothing I can do to fix it. Hell, I'd be lucky if she even keeps working for the company at this point. I was cruel. I said things I shouldn't have, and it's no one's fault but my own. I went from feeling nothing to feeling the whole range of emotions in one night: desire, lust, arousal, connection, jealousy, fear, denial, and anger. Fuck, why didn't I get a hold of myself?

I shove my hand through my hair in frustration and turn around to go to my truck. I get in and slam my hands down on the steering wheel.

I lied to her, and it's not a lie I can come back from. I told her that I wanted to sink my dick into a hot piece of ass like that was my plan all along. The truth is, I came into town knowing that I'd be going home alone tonight. I haven't been interested in a woman in I don't know how long. I wasn't looking for anything tonight, but it sure did hit me upside the head.

In the span of just a few minutes in her company, I was hooked and wanting more. I wanted more time, more talking, more kissing, more all of it.

And I fucked it up.

I count to ten and try to calm my nerves. Before I let myself follow her, I ram the gear shift in reverse and pull out of my parking spot. The tires squeal as I gun the gas and pull out onto the road leading up the mountain. It's only twenty minutes to my cabin in the woods, but it takes even less time tonight.

I wanted her. Hell, even now, my dick is still at half-mast just thinking about her. And I freaked out. I shouldn't have said what I said or did what I did, but even knowing all that, I know that there's no future between Maggie and me, so why even try? No, it's better this way. She's better off not getting involved with me or knowing how fucked-up I am. This is for the best.

But even knowing all that, I still can't seem to get her out of my head.

My phone rings as I park in front of my cabin. When I see it's my sister, I want to ignore it, but I know I can't. Something could be wrong with her or with Maggie.

"Yeah?" I answer as I get out of the truck and trudge toward my front door.

"Where's Maggie? The last I saw of her, she was walking outside after you, and she hasn't come back since." She pauses and in a hushed tone asks, "Oh my God, did she leave with you?"

"What? No, she didn't leave with me. She should be there at the office. I saw her walk back inside."

My sister's voice rises. "Ben! This is not like her. She wouldn't just leave. She's responsible and always does what she's supposed to do. She wouldn't just bail without telling someone."

I turn on my heel, ready to get back in my truck to go find her. "I'll come back into town. Give me fifteen minutes."

"Wait! I have a text," she says, and her voice is muffled as she takes the phone from her mouth. "Oh, she's home. She said she had a migraine... she's lying. If she's with you there, Ben, it's fine. I won't be mad; I just need to know she's okay."

I blow out a breath as I pace next to my truck, debating if I need to head back into town or not. "She's not with me. And how do you know she's lying? Maybe she does have a migraine." I swallow hard before I ask the next question. "Where's Cole? That was her date's name, right?"

Impatiently, Elana huffs. "Cole is here dancing with Clara from accounting, and the reason I know she's lying is because she gets migraines all the time, and they are bad. There's no way she was able to drive with one."

I get into my truck and start to head back down the mountain. With the Bluetooth on, I tell her, "Send me her address. I'm going to go by her house and make sure she's home."

"What? No, it's okay. I'm closer. I'll just leave here and go by her house real quick."

"No!" I yell into the cab of my truck. "I'm already on my way. What does she drive? I'll let you know if I see her car outside."

"Oooh, good idea. Okay. I'll send it to you. Thank you, Ben. You're a good man."

I wince at the guilt her words bring because I'm not a good man. If anything, from my actions earlier tonight, I'm a pretty shitty man actually. "I'll let you know," I answer her gruffly before hitting disconnect on my dash.

Shortly after hanging up, Elana's text comes through. Maggie's house is at the base of the mountain, and it won't take me long to get there. I feel as if I hold my breath the whole way into town. I pull to the side of the road in front of her house, and sure enough, her little Honda is parked in the driveway. I shut off my engine and pull my phone from the cupholder to send my sister a text. "She's home. Her car is in the driveway and there's a light on inside."

"Thank God. Thank you again, Ben. She texted me that she was fine and going to bed. I'm sorry... it's just not like her, and I freaked out a little. Thanks for helping me out."

"Sure, no problem. I'm going home. You did good tonight, sis. Love you."

I drop my phone into the cupholder and look at the small house where Maggie is inside, probably cursing my name as I sit here. I should drive away, but I don't. I stare up at her house for the longest time, wishing I hadn't said what I said earlier and that things were different. For the first time in a long time, I wonder what life would be like if I could open my heart again.

MAGGIE

I order a shot of whiskey. It's either that or I know Elana's going to give me a hard time about being a stick in the mud. Usually, I can withstand her peer pressure, but with the talk we're about to have, I need a little bit of liquid courage.

"Ooooh, whiskey. It's that kind of night? I'll take one too," she says excitedly.

I laugh and watch as the bartender pours our drinks and slides the glasses in front of us. In one gulp, without any fanfare, I throw back the shot that burns the whole way down my throat.

Elana is a little slower, and when she sets the half empty glass down, her face is puckered up. "I swear, that's like drinking fire. Why would you order that?"

I shrug, not ready to drop my bombshell just yet.

For one second, I thought I'd keep it to myself, but I tell Elana everything. Well, everything except the kiss and words I exchanged with her brother a few weeks ago. Nope, I've kept that all to myself.

But this... this is big, and I know I need to talk to her about it. I need to tell someone, and who else would I tell if not my best friend?

"So there's this guy..." she starts, and I cut her off.

I hold my hand up. "Nope, not interested."

She was searching on her phone, probably trying to find a picture to show me, but I cover her hand with mine, blocking the screen. "Forget it, Elana. I'm not going to let you hook me up."

For just an instant, the image of Ben with his dark eyes and long beard filter through my brain, and I have to force the memories out. "But I do have something I need to talk to you about."

She lays her phone down on the bar top. "Shoot. You have my full attention."

I take a deep breath. "I need Friday off... I need a long weekend."

Her eyes round in surprise. "Sure, I mean you have worked overtime every week since you started with the company. Of course you can take a day off if you need it."

I wring my hands together and then pull them

back to hold in my lap. It's obvious I'm nervous, and Elana will notice before anyone. She squints her eyes and looks at me. "What are you hiding?"

I lift my shoulders and force a smile to my face. "I'm not hiding anything."

She rolls her eyes. "Fine. What are you not telling me?"

My forehead creases, but I ignore her question. "I know that we are catering the alcohol for the mayor's party on Monday night. I'll still be able to attend and cover it for social media."

She's staring straight at me. "I know you don't shirk your responsibilities, Maggie. I'm not worried about it. Now let's get back to why you need the day off."

I force a laugh. "Geez, can't a girl get a day off without getting the third degree?"

Elana leans forward. "Absolutely. If Paula in HR asked for the day off, she could have it no questions asked. Rachel, Emma, Clara, Terry... same. But when my best friend asks for the day off and is being all secretive about it, I'm going to ask. So what's up? What are you doing?"

I shrug and still don't answer her. It's not that I don't want to; it's just that I don't know how to word it.

She takes another sip of her drink and scrunches her nose as she swallows. "Fine. You know what? I need some time off too. Maybe I'll take off, and we can do whatever it is you're hiding together."

I lean back in my seat. "I'm not hiding it. I'm going to tell you, but I don't know how to say it. I don't want you to judge me, that's all."

She crosses her arms over her chest. "You're worried about me judging you? Do you remember the time you had to sneak me out of the Theta fraternity house to avoid the walk of shame? Or the time I drank too much, and you had to clean vomit out of my hair? I mean, I can go on, but the point is, I'm the last person to judge anyone. Especially you."

I know she's right. I reach into my purse and pull out the printed copy of the invitation from my email. I bite my lip as I slide it across to her.

She grabs it up with a flourish and starts to read. The smile that's on her face slowly drops, and she's loud when she holds the paper up between us. "No fucking way, Maggie."

I grab the paper from her hand and stuff it back into my purse. "You said you wouldn't judge me."

She shakes her head. "I'm not, but this isn't you. Why would you do that?"

"Why would I auction off my virginity? Well, let's

see. I'm twenty-three years old, and I'm sick of dating. It's turned into this big ole thing now, and I just want to get it over with."

She sputters. "Well, that's a crazy reason. You could just hook up at a bar or something. You don't have to"—she leans in and whispers—"you know, sell yourself."

I rear back, surprised. "You're judging me!" I accuse her.

She's shaking her head. "No, I'm not. I'm not judging you at all. I just don't understand. Is it the money? If that's the case, I can lend it to you."

I cross my arms over my chest. "A million dollars will be nice, but no, it's not the money. I just... I need to do this."

I can't explain it to her. Mostly because she doesn't know the whole story. I wonder what she would think if she knew that I wanted to go home with her brother recently. That I'd only known him for less than an hour and I was dry humping him in the courtyard at work. Or the fact that he's all I've thought about since. I feel as if I'm going crazy. You would think after what he said to me, it would be easy to dismiss him, but I haven't been able to get him off my mind. This auction invitation came at the right time. Elana doesn't know it, but the only man I want I can't have. I need to do this.

She tilts her head as she searches my eyes. I know she's trying to figure this out. Auctioning myself off is not something I would normally do. She's justified in her surprise. I hold my hand up. "I'm not losing it or going crazy. I'm just ready. I don't want to date or do all that. Trust me... you know me, Elana. I've thought about this carefully and weighed all the pros and cons. There are safety procedures in place. Everyone has to be vetted; it's not just a free-for-all. I promise you I wouldn't do this if I had any doubts at all. I want to do it."

She still doesn't look happy about it, but at least she gives up trying to change my mind. "Okay, give me all the details, and don't leave anything out."

I spend the next thirty minutes telling her everything I know about it. She taps the bar top with her knuckles. "Wait. There's a marriage option? You could get married this weekend?"

I bark out a laugh. "How come I feel like you're more worried about getting cheated out of your spot as maid of honor than you are about me actually getting married?"

She laughs with me as she orders two more drinks.

"You know me well. So what? Are you telling me you may get married this weekend?"

"No, I'm not getting married. It's an option, but both people have to agree to it, and I'm definitely not binding myself to someone that I just met." No sooner are the words out than I start thinking of Ben. Damn, why can't I stop thinking about him?

Elana lets out a breath. "Good. It's one thing to have sex with someone you just met, but marriage is like forever..."

I nod in agreement.

Elana slides my drink to me and lifts up her own glass. "All right, let's drink." She holds the glass toward me. "To your virginity."

I set my arm down on the bar. "Really? That's what you want to drink to?"

She throws her head back and laughs. "Well, just think about it. This time next week, we won't be able to drink to it, so if you ask me, it's a pretty good toast."

I can see her logic, even if it is a little weird. "Fine." I raise my glass and clink it to hers. "To my virginity."

I gulp down the shot while she chimes in, "Oooh, and hoping you get a man that knows what a clit is."

I choke on the shot of whiskey, and Elana starts to hoot with laughter. The people around us are all staring, but it doesn't faze me. I give in to the moment and laugh with her. We laugh until our sides hurt and our cheeks are aching. For the first time in weeks, I'm happy. I've told my best friend my plan, and I'm one day closer to doing this auction and hopefully forgetting about the brooding, bearded Ben.

BEN

"Are you coming next Monday night?"

I raise my eyebrows and look at my sister Elana with my fork halfway to my mouth. We're having our weekly dinner, and she's only been here ten minutes and already she's trying to talk me into going to town. "To the mayor's shindig?"

She nods around the mouth full of spaghetti.

I take the bite and shake my head.

"Why not?"

I give her the look. The one that says *Don't ask me stupid questions*. Plus, there's no way I can go to that event because I know that Maggie will be there. She's been talking about it for the past week on her social media, so I'm sure she'll be in attendance. And I already feel that I'm hanging on a ledge here. I really fucked things up with her. I shake my head to try and get the memories out of my head once and for all and direct my attention to my sister. "So what's up? What's new in your life?"

She scrunches her nose up. "Really? Nothing is new. All I do is work. I need a vacation."

I look down at my plate and move the food around. "Well, do it. Take a vacation."

She shrugs, and I've tried to hold off, but I can't resist any longer. "I've been getting notifications from the Moonshine Mountain social media accounts. Your new social media girl seems to be doing a really good job."

"Who? Maggie? She's not new. Not really. She's worked for us for over a year now, but yeah, she's good. She has a real knack for that stuff."

I hold back the groan. A year she's been right under my nose, and I had no idea.

I listen to her talk about her best friend, and I'm quiet, hoping that she goes on. "She's smart, Ben. I wish I was that smart."

"You're smart too."

She snorts. "Not Maggie smart. She is just something else. She wants something, she goes for it. She works all the time, never takes any time off. Well, I mean, she asked for Friday off, but that will be her first day she's missed since she started."

I lean forward and try to act nonchalant even though I can feel my blood pressure rising. "Oh yeah? What did she need the day off for? You two have plans?"

Elana laughs again. "Nope, not this time. Trust me, you wouldn't want me to do this with her."

"What is she doing?" I ask her sharply.

Elana realizes then that she's said too much. "Nothing. I mean, really, it's none of our business. She never takes time off, and she's taking one day. I approved it."

I squint my eyes at her. "What is she doing, Elana?"

She gets up, taking her plate to the sink. "I told you, she's taking the day off."

I get up and follow her. "Yeah, but you're acting all weird about it."

She bursts out with a fake laugh before going back to the table and grabbing my plate. She won't look at me, and that's the best indication that something is up. "You do know she works for Moonshine Mountain. If she's in trouble... or if she needs something, we should—"

"You wash and I'll dry," she answers, thinking I'm going to drop it.

I start washing the dishes, but I don't stop. "So does she need help? Is she okay?"

Elana takes the plate from my hands and dries it. "She's fine. She's responsible, and she says she knows what she's doing. Plus, why do you care? You met her one time."

It's on the tip of my tongue to tell her that even though I met her that one time, I haven't been able to get her off my mind, but I don't say it. Instead, I hustle through the dishes. It's obvious that I'm not going to get any information from my sister. I'm going to have to find out what's going on my own way.

No sooner do we finish dishes than Elana says she needs to get back into town. I'm standing in the doorway of my cabin as she drives off. As soon as she waves at me in the rearview mirror, I'm heading to my home office and logging into my computer.

What are you up to, Maggie?

First, I look at the camera that I installed outside her house. Even now, I feel like a creep for doing it, but I justified it to myself that I just wanted to make sure she got home safe at night. I've spent hours the last few weeks watching her come and go or sit on her front porch swing and read a book. Her car is home, so whatever she's doing, she hasn't left yet.

Next, I log into the Distillery's mainframe. This I feel less guilty about. It's the company email, and it's monitored anyway. Why can't I log in to her email just to see what she's got planned? I try to convince myself it's for her safety, but after forty minutes of searching, I don't find anything out of the ordinary.

I debate with myself for all of fifteen minutes before I make my next move. It's a complete invasion of privacy, but there's no way I can go another minute without knowing what she's up to.

I connect to my hacker software and put it to work. Within two minutes, it has me logged into Maggie's personal email. I feel sick to my stomach because I know I shouldn't be doing this. It's wrong on so many levels, but even knowing that doesn't stop me.

The subject line *You're invited to the Breeder's Auction House* pops out to me, and I click on it.

She was invited to an elite auction. I've heard of it before but only in passing. I read the details, and Maggie is invited to auction off her virginity for one million dollars. I hold on to my breath and click on her sent folder. I scan the emails until I see it. She responded to the invitation.

As I read the email, my palms get sweaty, and my heart feels as if it's going to pound out of my chest. She signed the contract. Maggie... the woman that I can't forget. The woman that I'm obsessed with and that I pushed away is auctioning off her virginity. I stand up over my computer, hands on the desk, leaning over like I'm ready to pounce. "No!" I scream. She can't do it. There's no way I can let her do this. What is she thinking?

I push everything off the top of my desk and sling it to the floor. Enraged, I stomp through the cabin until I'm outside and I can't hold back any longer. The sound that erupts from me doesn't even sound human. It's filled with rage. Panting, I pace back and forth, trying to catch my breath. My thoughts are everywhere, but one thing I know for sure: When she does this, when she stands on that stage to auction herself off, I'll be the one that wins... no matter the cost.

MAGGIE

I'm next.

I've almost talked myself out of this a hundred times, but whenever I think about Ben, I know I'm doing the right thing. I don't know why I'm hung up on him, but I'm positive doing this will finally clear all remnants of him from my head. It has to.

I don't know what kind of hold he has on me. I met him, and thirty minutes later, I was ready to have sex with him. Three weeks later, I can't get him off my mind. I shake my head. Geez, imagine if I actually had slept with him. I'd probably be obsessed.

This whole thing has been overwhelming. From the moment I got here to the site of the auction, I've been plucked and prodded. I have more makeup on than I've ever worn in my life, and I'm basically parading around this place in my underwear.

The owner of the auction, Coco St James, has bossed me and everyone else around, but I have to admit, it runs like a well-oiled machine.

"Now here's a special treat. We have lucky number seven."

I grit my teeth when they call my number, but I force my shaky legs to take me out onto the stage. The audience is dark, and I can't see a thing, which makes this a little easier. I try to convince myself that no one is out there as I walk to the end of the stage and turn back around. My hands are straight at my sides as I try to hold down my see-through lingerie. My ass is bare, and I know I'm showing it with each step I take. Coco St. James rambles on about me, but it's like a whoosh of air in my ear because I don't make out anything she says. I'm full of nerves and trying not to bolt the whole time I stand here.

"Let's start the bidding at one million."

There's a buzz in the room, and Coco smiles. "Well, okay, everyone. Someone is obviously smitten. I have a bid for five million. Can I get five and a half?"

I gasp, but before I can react, there are more buzzes in the room. Each one makes the bid go higher, and when Coco St. James calls the final bid at eight million dollars, I feel faint.

Someone just bought my virginity for eight million dollars.

The reality of what I'm doing hits me like a punch in the gut. I stumble off the stage, and a security guard leads me to a side room. I wait impatiently for my buyer to come, and when Bentley Barrett walks through the door, I feel a mix of relief and anger at the same time.

"No," I say as soon as I spot him.

His eyes travel down the length of me, and my traitorous body reacts. My nipples pucker, and there's a pull in my lower belly. Damn, he's handsome. Even more so than I remember.

"What are you doing here?"

He walks to the counter that's been set up. "What does it look like I'm doing?"

I cross my arms over my chest. "I'm not leaving with you."

He lifts his hand and strokes it through his beard while he looks at me. "Yes, you are. Because I'm not leaving you here."

The man at the counter clears his throat. "Ma'am, you signed the contract. If you have changed your mind, you will need to talk to Coco about it." I'm about to nod my head when he continues, "But you'd be wasting your time. Unless you have eight million dollars, the contract is binding. Of course, you're free to do whatever, but you will be the one paying the bill."

Eight million dollars. I don't have eight million dollars. Heck, I don't even have eight thousand dollars. "Fine," I say.

Ben transfers the money, and when the cashier asks if we want the marriage option, I tell him no, absolutely not.

Ben doesn't look at me. He doesn't seem happy, and I can't say I blame him.

We finally get out the door, and Ben is leading me to his truck. As I climb in, I ask him, "Did Elana send you?"

He slams the door and walks around to the driver's side and gets in. "No, Elana didn't send me."

I dig through my bag and pull my phone out. I dial Elana's number, and she answers on the first ring. "You okay?"

Instead of answering her, I ask my own question. "Why did you send your brother to get me?"

She gasps. "Eddie's there?"

"No, Ben is here."

She's quiet for a second and then blurts out, "Ben is there? My brother Ben... is at the auction?"

My voice drops a little. Elana is good, but she really does sound like she doesn't have a clue what's going on. "Yes. Ben is here, and he bid on me."

"He what?"

I look over at Ben, and he's holding on to the steering wheel with white knuckles. "You didn't know?"

Elana gasps into the phone. "No, I didn't know. How did he even know you were there? I didn't tell him."

"I'll call you back," I tell her and then hang up.

I turn in my seat and face him. "What is going on, Ben? Why did you come?"

He enunciates each word. "Because I wasn't going to let you sell yourself to some stranger, that's why."

"What do you care? You hate me."

His rigid jaw softens along with his voice. "I don't hate you."

"Right. I'm just a hot piece of ass to you." He doesn't say anything, but I'm not going to stop until I get to the bottom of this. "How did you know... oh shit, you were there to bid on someone. You saw me and felt you needed to save me or something. You were there for someone else."

He looks at me with a tight expression on his face. "No."

Exasperated, I throw my hand up. "No what?"

He turns back to the road in front of us. "No, I wasn't there for someone else."

My body quivers. If he wasn't there for someone else, does that mean he really was there for me? No. There's no way. "Why then?"

His voice is hard. "Because I wasn't going to stand by while you sold yourself to some stranger. Fuck, Maggie. You have no idea how much I hated seeing you up there."

Has he thought of me at all these last few weeks? Is he doing this because I work for him? Why does he care when all he wanted was a piece of ass?

I cringe at the thought that comes next. "Does everyone at work know?"

He grits his teeth. "No."

"So if no one knows, and Elana didn't tell you, how did you know I was there?"

He blows out a breath as he stops at a stop sign. "You're not going to like it, Maggie."

He starts to drive again, and I turn in my seat with one hand on the dashboard. "I'm not going to like it? What does that even mean?"

He shrugs. "It means you're not going to like it."

"Ben! Stop this. I'm tired of these games. How did you know about this?"

He keeps his eyes on the road. "Elana came to dinner the other night and told me you were going on vacation, but she wouldn't tell me where. I was worried about you, and I had to know." He takes a deep breath and lets it out slowly. "I looked at your email."

I think back to the invitation I'd received and the application I sent back. "My email? Wait, that was my personal email."

He looks at me almost guiltily. "I know."

"You looked at my personal email? How did you even do that? Why would you do that?"

He doesn't answer me, though. We're at the main intersection in town, and Ben turns toward the distilleries. I point the opposite direction. "I live that way."

"I know where you live."

I shake my head. "Of course you do. Where are you going? Take me home."

He keeps driving, seemingly unfazed. "I'm taking you home with me."

I laugh. How can I not? This whole thing is crazy. "I'm not going home with you."

"Yes, you are."

I wave my hand in his face. "Uh, hello. No, I'm not."

"Yes, you are. I have eight million reasons saying you are."

I gulp. I never thought.... I didn't think that he actually wanted to follow through on this. "Ben, surely you don't think—"

"I'm not going to force you to sleep with me. You don't have anywhere to be until Monday. Stay with me."

Fuck, I want to. I want to stay with him more than anything, but does that make me weak? He only wants me for one thing. But he did pay eight million dollars to get it. I look over at him and can't help but wonder what's going on in his head. He could have literally had me for free. "None of this makes sense."

He shrugs and keeps driving up the mountain. "It will."

I put my hand on his forearm and feel his muscles flex under my palm. He's affected by my touch. "Why? Give me one good reason... Why should I?"

There's torment in his eyes. "Because I messed up. That day I met you, I fucked up. I want to make it right."

I cross my arms over my chest. I can feel myself softening to him, but I'm trying to keep my wits about me. "Fine, you want to be forgiven? You're forgiven. You could have saved eight million dollars and just picked up the phone to apologize to me. You don't spend that kind of money to make something right, Ben."

"Will you go with me or not?"

I bite my lower lip. "I'm not fucking you."

His eyes drop to my lips before looking back at the road. "That's your decision. I would like for you to stay, Maggie."

I should demand he take me home, but I don't. Instead, I turn and sit straight in my seat and look out the side window. "Fine," I mutter. "I'll go home with you."

I don't have to look at him to see his reaction. I can see the smile on his face through the reflection of the glass. I hope I'm making the right decision.

BEN

She agreed to come home with me. I thought she would refuse me, so I press on the gas a little harder to get us home faster.

She's quiet the rest of the ride, and when I pull into my driveway, I try to look at my cabin through her eyes and imagine what she's seeing. To me, it's my sanctuary, but what will she think about it?

I've only ever had my brother and sister here, so it's hard to know how someone else would see it.

I grab her bag, and she gets out of the truck before I can come around to help her. She doesn't trust me. I can't see it by the way she's glaring at me, and I can't say I blame her. I pushed her away, and I invaded her privacy. I'm going to have to earn her trust back.

As we walk toward the cabin, I'm watching her as

she looks up at the one-story house in front of us. She likes it. Her eyes are sparkling, and there's a soft smile on her face, letting me know she approves. I don't know why it means that much to me, but it does.

I open the front door and show her around the cabin. It's an open concept, and I point out the different rooms. She's quiet as she takes it all in. I walk across the room to the door that leads to the guest room. I would love if she would share a bed with me, but I know I'd be pushing it. "This is your room."

She reaches for the bag that's in my hands, and I let her take it. She walks into the room and slams the door in my face.

I scrub my hand across my face. Fuck, I need a drink.

I walk into the kitchen and pour a small shot of whiskey into a glass. As I swirl the amber liquid around, I think back to seeing her on that stage. I've never felt so attracted to someone in my life. I'd barely noticed the woman that went before her, but it's like my body knew when she would be walking out. The other men in the room wanted her too. I knew they would, but I also knew that I wouldn't be leaving without her. I would have bid whatever I had to bid to have this opportunity with her. All I want is to claim her and make her mine.

She's not happy with me at all, though. I know I have a lot of explaining to do, but she's not in any mood to listen to me. *Fuck, what if she leaves?*

My feet carry me across the house before I can think better of it. I knock on her door and stand impatiently waiting for her. She cracks open the door and looks up at me. "What?"

"Promise me you won't leave. I mean, promise you won't try and walk off this mountain. It's dangerous."

She leans against the doorjamb. "Well, then don't give me a reason to if you're so worried about it, Ben."

She's so beautiful as she looks up at me. The need to pull her into my arms is strong. "I know I don't have a right to ask you this…"

She licks her lips. "What?"

Fuck, I feel like a schoolboy, but I know I need to take it slowly with her. "Can I kiss you?"

She bites her lip. She wants to say yes. Her eyes get darker, and her breath hitches. "I said…"

I cut her off and push the door open a little farther. "I know what you said. I'm not asking you to sleep with me. I'm asking you for a kiss, that's all."

Her knuckles are white as she grips the door. I prepare myself that she's probably going to say no, but I'm surprised when she starts to nod her head. "Sure, why not?"

As soon as she says yes, I lean down. She raises on her tiptoes, and when her lips touch mine, a feeling of complete satisfaction overwhelms me. Ever since that kiss a few weeks ago, I'd wondered if maybe it was a fluke and that it was just the night or the emotions I was feeling then. But with her lips on mine, I know that there is something between us. I wrap my hand around the base of her neck and tilt my head to the side to deepen the kiss. My tongue strokes against hers, and the sound of her moan has me stopping and pulling back.

I'm breathing as if I've just run a mile as I search her eyes. She feels it, too. I know she does.

"I knew it."

She blinks up at me in a daze. "You knew what?"

"I knew when I kissed you before that you were different. I fucked up, Maggie. But you have to know there's something between us. You have to feel it.

She wants to believe me. The hope in her eyes is so evident it's almost blinding. "But…"

I shake my head "But nothing. Admit it… you feel something for me."

And just like that, her face drops. "I did. A few weeks ago in that courtyard at work, I felt something. Hell, Ben, I was ready to give myself to you then, and you pushed me away."

"I told you that I fucked up."

She moves back into her room and says, "Yeah, you did. And you could have fixed it. You could have made it right. Instead, you made me feel like I wasn't good enough for you and left. I'm done talking now."

I put my arm across the door to block her from shutting it. "But..."

She holds her hand up. "I'm done. Please, let me shower. You didn't like seeing me up there? Imagine how I felt."

Before I can ask her why she was even there, I let her close the door in my face. I lean my head against the cool, hard wood. I have to make this right one way or another. She's going to leave here on Monday, and somehow I need to make things right before then. If I have my way, I'm going to do my best to convince her to stay.

MAGGIE

After a really hot shower, I get dressed in a pair of shorts and a T-shirt. I pace across the bedroom, ignoring the rumbling in my stomach. I can smell the Italian spices coming from the kitchen, and it's reminding me that I haven't eaten all day.

I know I need to go out there and face Ben. I'm so confused about everything, but the more I think about it, the more I come to terms with it. Regardless of whatever took place three weeks ago, the fact is he spent eight million dollars for me. That has to mean something.

I walk out to the kitchen and stand awkwardly. I probably should have done something with myself.

"You feel better?" he asks, looking at me from head

to toe.

I nod and move farther into the room. "Yeah, I think I scraped off three inches of makeup."

He walks next to me and sets two plates on the table. He looks at me up close, and a soft smile forms on his lips. "You're beautiful, Maggie."

Heat forms on my face, and I smile. "Can I help with anything?"

"No, it's ready. Have a seat."

I sit down while he brings everything to the table. He dishes me out some spaghetti, and I dig in. We eat in silence for a while, and I try to slow down, but it's really good.

It takes me a minute before I realize he's not touching his food but instead just watching me.

I cover my mouth and swallow. "What?"

He shrugs. "I like watching you."

I laugh. "You like watching me stuff my face?"

His hands curl against the hard wood of the table. "I like watching you enjoy your food. You make the cutest sounds and expressions."

I put my fork down and cover my face. "Oh God, I probably shouldn't eat in public."

He reaches over and wraps his hand around mine, pulling it down. "Don't stop. Did you eat anything today?"

I shake my head. "No. I was too nervous."

He blinks, and it's obvious he has something on his mind. "Go ahead. You have something you want to say. You might as well get it off your chest."

He nods. "Why did you do the auction? Is it the money?"

I shake my head. "No—I mean, don't get me wrong, the money is nice, but that's not why I did it."

"Why then? Why did you do it?"

I answer his question with a question of my own. "Why am I here?"

He juts out his chin. "You tell me why you decided to do the auction, and I'll tell you why I went and bid for you. No bullshit."

I nod. "Okay. Here's the truth. I felt I didn't have a choice. I felt like I was going crazy. There's... a man... he's not interested in me... he's unavailable. I couldn't get him out of my head, and I thought by doing this... giving myself to someone and finally losing my virginity, I could move on."

His jaw is so tight it looks as if it might shatter. His eyes are staring back at me hard. He's mad, but it doesn't stop me from asking him, "Your turn. Why did you spend eight million dollars on me when you could have had me for free?"

He's glaring at me now, and I'm waiting for him to

storm out. He looks as if he's about to bolt, but there's no way I'm going to let that happen. Not again.

"Ben, you said you'd tell me. Now why am I here? Some misplaced guilt, trying to protect your company? What is it?"

He rears back in surprise. "You think I did this to protect Moonshine Distilleries?"

I shrug, not knowing what to think anymore. "Honestly, I'm not sure why. I've tried to look at it from every angle, but I'm not sure. Why were you there, Ben? Why am I here?"

"I told you that I read your email and knew you would be there. I went because I wanted to be there, and I was going to be the winning bid."

My voice rises in frustration. "But why?"

"Because for the past few weeks, all I've thought about is you. I wanted you then, and..."

I interrupt him. "And you walked away."

He leans forward, his face inches from mine. "For a reason. I walked away for a reason. I didn't want to."

He gets up, and I do too. "Don't walk away, Ben."

He stops, and understanding crosses his face. He leans toward me and kisses my forehead. "I'm just going to grab something. I'll be right back."

I watch him go wondering what he's up to. When

he comes back, he's carrying something that he got off the mantle.

He hands a picture frame to me, and I look at it. I trace the little boy's face with my fingers. He's an adorable kid. "Who is this, Ben?"

"His name is Benji. He..."

Ben's voice breaks off, and I move toward him. I have one hand on the picture frame, and the other reaches for him. Obviously, this is hard for him. I've never seen a man so physically shaken before. "You don't have to—"

He cuts me off. "Yeah, I do. I need to explain." He lets out a rough breath. "I haven't talked about this in years."

There's a huskiness in his voice, filled with emotion. "That's Benji. Uh, I was married to his mother. For a year, I thought I was his father. He was my son. He will always be my son, even though I never get to see him anymore."

I shake my head in confusion. "Wait, what are you saying?"

"She cheated on me but let me think that Benji was mine. I probably would still think he was mine if she hadn't found another sucker that has more money than me."

I gasp in shock. My hands go to his waist. "I'm so sorry, Ben. I can't even imagine how that felt."

His hands go to my shoulders, and his fingers trail up and down the sides of my neck. "It was awful. Losing Benji—I don't think I'll ever get over that."

I cup his jaw. "One day, when he's older, he'll want to see you, and she'll have to let him."

He blinks, and hope shines in his eyes before it quickly fades. "He was one. He won't remember me."

All I can do is look at him, and things start to fit together. Elana had mentioned his past and trying to get over something. I couldn't imagine being in his position. That had to have almost killed him. And then the betrayal of his wife had to destroy him. "Ben..." I start, but he doesn't let me finish.

"When I saw you in the courtyard at work, it was the first time I'd felt anything in years. Talking to you, kissing you, touching you, I forgot about old hurts and was ready for more. Then when we walked out and Elana said your date was there, I thought the worst. Add that to the fact that I didn't know you were so young and you're my little sister's best friend, I freaked out. Everything I was feeling... I knew that there was no way you were feeling the same way. In that instant, I freaked out."

BEN

She wraps her arms around my neck like she's afraid I'm going to walk away or something. She doesn't realize that I'm done with all that. I fucked up, but I won't make the same mistake again.

I put my hands at her waist, pulling her flush against me as she begins to talk. "I didn't go on a date with Cole. Elana is always trying to fix me up. Honestly, I forgot that she had even tried to fix me up with someone until she reminded me that night. But I'm not the type to date more than one man."

I nod and squeeze her. "I know that now."

She looks up at me through her lashes. "When I met you, I wasn't thinking anything. I wanted to kiss you, though. I wanted to go home with you, and I've never felt that way with anyone else... I've thought about that night ever since then. I wondered what went wrong and why you reacted the way you did. I didn't know you were the Ben Barrett. I wasn't targeting you."

I shake my head softly. "I didn't think you did. I realize now that I messed up and overreacted. I'm sorry, Maggie. I really am."

She nods. "It's fine." She pulls back, and I'm forced to let her go. She wraps her arms around her waist and stares up at me. She has no idea that I can see every thought and every doubt on her face. She's not sure she can trust me.

"I want to give you the whole truth, Maggie. I need to come clean."

She swallows and grabs the chair next to her. "Okay. I'm listening."

I take a step toward her, but I don't touch her. We're mere inches from each other, close enough I can feel the heat from her body, but I don't touch her. "I'm giving you the whole truth right now, and I need you to hear me out."

She looks at me worriedly, probably wondering what bombshell I'm about to drop on her. "I'm obsessed with you, Maggie. Since that day, I haven't thought of anyone but you. I followed you on social media just to get a glimpse into your life, but it wasn't enough." I take a deep breath, knowing I need to tell her the whole truth. "I installed cameras outside your house so I could see you come and go. The cameras in the office were my idea, and I watch you walk up and down the hall, all day every day. When I found out you were doing the auction, I couldn't sit by anymore."

She asks me breathlessly, "You stalk me?"

I cringe. "I would never hurt you. And you know why I do it."

She tilts her head to the side, and her eyes light up. "You want me?"

I can feel the blood coursing through my veins, and my voice drops an octave. "Oh yeah, Maggie. I want you."

She leans toward me, and I have to ask. I may not have the right, but I need to know. "The man that you think you can't have—"

Her hands slide up my chest. "It's you, Ben. You're the one I thought I couldn't have."

My body trembles. "I'm yours, honey. Since the day I first saw you, I've been yours."

She wraps her hand around my neck and pulls me down as she goes on her tiptoes. "You can have me, Ben."

A shudder passes through me. I lean down and put one arm behind her back and one behind her legs before lifting her up to cradle against me. She comes to me easily and rests her hand on my chest. I don't move. I can't because just having her in my arms is fulfilling.

She gives me a little slap on my chest. "Now what, Mr. Barrett? What are you going to do with me now?"

That brings me out of my trance. I stalk across the house to carry her to my bedroom. "If I was a better man, I'd tell you that we can wait until you're ready, but I'm dying for you. Instead, I'm going to spend the rest of the weekend making you forget how much pain I've caused you."

She kisses my chest. "It's okay, really. I understand why you did..."

I stand her on her feet next to my bed. "It doesn't make it right."

She gets a smile on her face and sits down on the bed before sliding to the middle. My hands fist at my sides the farther she moves away from me. The only reprieve I have is knowing it's my bed she's in.

She holds her hands up to me. "I know how you can make it up to me."

My hips surge forward just thinking about everything I want to do to her.

I follow her path along the bed and hover over her. I want to touch and taste every part of her.

She pulls at the T-shirt she's wearing. "Should I take this off?"

I reach for the hem. "Let me."

She sits up, and I pull the shirt up her body. By the time it's off, I'm already panting. Her breasts are large and rounded and jiggle with every breath. I mold my palm to her, plucking her hard peaks through the shear bra with my fingers. "Off. I need to see all of you."

I undo the front clasp of her bra, and her breasts bounce when they are unbound. I can't hold back. I lean forward, pressing my lips to her, suckling her.

She arches her back, pushing herself to get closer to me. I'm touching every inch of bare skin I can reach.

Her fingers tunnel through my hair before gripping the back of my head and holding me to her. She pleads with me. "Ben, please, it's not enough. I need all of you. I want to feel your body against mine. Please."

I pull back and take in three deep, dragging breaths.

I could come right now, but I won't let myself. No, my pleasure won't come until she's fully satisfied and completely hooked on what I can give her.

I lean forward and kiss her lips. She pulls me on top of her, and I try to hold my weight off her so I don't hurt her, but she pulls her lips from mine. "Please, Ben. Don't hold back."

I lean my forehead against her heaving chest. Fuck, this is too much.

"Let me take my clothes off."

It's an excuse to put some distance between us, but it works because she releases her hold on me. I move off the bed and stand next to it. Quickly, I remove my shirt and then my pants. My cock is hard and pulsating.

I swipe my finger on my tip, smearing the precum along my head.

She leans across the bed and reaches for my hand, pulling it to her mouth. When she brings my finger to her mouth, sucking off the evidence of my desire, it takes everything I have to stay rooted in my spot.

She pops off my finger with a smack of her lips. Her eyes are bright, and she smiles at me. "More. I want more."

Her hand goes to my hip, and she pulls me to her. There's no way I can resist her, even though I know this is a bad idea. As soon as she puts her lips to my manhood, my hips surge.

"Fuck," I groan breathlessly as I put my hand on her shoulder.

She smiles before opening her mouth and sticking out her tongue. She licks me from root to tip, and my head falls back.

She's relentless as she takes me in, stroking her tongue along my length.

Over and over, my hips pump gently until my whole body tenses. I'm close. Too close, and I know one more pump and I'll be coming down her throat. That's not where I want to be.

I pull my hips back, and she looks at me with a pout.

"Lie back," I order her.

She lies back, and I pull at the shorts she has on.

With a growl from me, she lifts her hips, and I pull her panties and shorts down her legs before tossing them across the room.

Her legs automatically fall open, and I climb onto the bed, using my shoulders to fit between her legs.

I kiss her inner thighs, and she lifts her hips.

Her hand goes to the back of my head, and I lick her from her hole to her clit.

Her moans fill the room, and I don't stop. My hips flex into the bed as I feast on her.

Her hips gyrate, pumping into my face as I kiss, lick, and suck her. I need her to come, and I need to hear her calling my name when she does it.

I pump my finger in and out of her as I circle her clit with my tongue. She releases her hold on my head, and her fingers dig into the sheets on the bed. Her body starts to jerk, and she writhes underneath me. Her whole body is taut as the orgasm shoots through her. She's begging me, but I don't stop. "One more. Give me one more, Maggie."

I increase the pressure, filling her with two fingers as her warm pussy grips on to me.

She bellows my name, thrusting up against me as another orgasm spears through her body. I keep lapping at her until she's lying limp on the bed.

MAGGIE

He crawls up my body, and I can feel his hard manhood against my hip. His precum is smeared across my skin, and I smile tiredly up at him. His lips and beard are coated with my release. "Uh, you have, uh, me all over your mouth."

His smile gets bigger, and he looks at me possessively. "I like having you all over me."

I loop my arms around his neck and pull him down to me. His lips meet mine, and I thought I'd be grossed out by the taste of myself on him, but honestly, it brings my desire to a whole other level.

I think it does the same for him. He groans as he pulls his mouth off mine and nuzzles against my neck. "Ben."

"Yeah, honey?"

"Are you... are we going to... you know?"

He lifts away from me far enough so he can see my face. "Fuck yeah. Honey, I don't plan on stopping until you're coming on my cock."

My face heats at his crude words but not because I'm embarrassed. It's like he knows exactly what I want.

I slide my leg from underneath him, and with a little wiggle, I have his hips encased with mine. I take a deep breath and hold it. "I'm ready."

His thumb grazes back and forth on my cheek. "You know if you don't want to do this..."

His voice trails off, but I know what he's thinking. He's wanting me to know that even though he paid for it, I don't have to have sex with him. Not if I'm not ready. But the truth is, I'm more than ready. Since the night I met him, I knew then he was the one what I wanted to be with. Of course, I imagined more than one night or in this case, more than one weekend, but there's no way I'm walking away now. I'd never forgive myself.

I reach down between us and wrap my hand around his hard girth. He's big, and I swear it gets even bigger as I hold on to him firmly. "I want this, Ben. I want you to be my first."

His hips surge, and he positions himself between my thighs. He grips on to my waist with one hand and wraps his other hand around himself. He strokes it once, and I move myself over, wanting to feel him inside me.

He strokes himself again, and I lift my hips to meet his. "Please," I beg him.

He slowly enters me and stops a few inches in. His hand pats me on my lower belly. "Breathe."

I let out a whoosh of air, and at the same time, he plunges into me in one big thrust. He fills me up. The pain is quick and swift, but I don't dwell on it. My eyes are glued to his, and he's watching me. He knows the instant I want more because he slowly starts to move inside me. In and out, he glides through my swollen, slick core.

It's too much. All of it is too much, and I clench my eyes shut as he gyrates in and out of me. My eyes pop open when he stops. "Don't—"

He cuts me off as he hovers over me. "I don't want to stop, but I need your eyes on me, Maggie."

I nod, and without blinking, I stare up at him.

It's like the look he's giving me is a whole story. In his eyes, I see everything he's wanting to say to me but doesn't put the words to. His hands grip my hips, and he pulls me up, hitting me in a different spot. My whole body responds to the pleasure that erupts inside me. My nails dig into his arms as he thrusts in and out of me. "Yes, oh fuck, Ben, yes." I scream gibberish to him, but it's like I can't form a coherent thought. I've never felt pleasure like this, and I don't want it to stop.

He's relentless as he drives into me. "Come for me, Maggie. Come on my cock."

The dirty words he's grunting at me along with the way his rod hits me in just the right spot puts me over the edge, and I do what he asks. My pussy spasms, clenching him as he erupts inside me with a loud bellow.

He falls down on top of me, and I wrap my arms and legs around him, holding him to me. He tries to wrench free and pull some of his weight off me, but I don't let him. "No, don't move yet."

He leans back enough to look at my face. "I need to clean you up. And you're going to be sore."

I rub my nose along his cheek with a sigh. "It was worth it."

I feel his cheek widen with a grin. "Fuck yeah, it was."

We both catch our breaths, lost in thought and wrapped in each other's arms. He reluctantly pulls out of me, and I grimace at the brief bout of pain. I thought I could hide my discomfort, but he notices it right away.

He grabs on to my arm and lifts me up into a sitting position. "Shower, let's go."

I want nothing more to curl up in his bed, but a hot shower is probably what I need right now. I follow him into the bathroom, and insecurity hits me in the face. After we shower, is he going to take me home? We didn't talk about afterward. Heck, we really didn't talk a lot about what's next, but I know that I don't want to ruin what we have going right now. Nope, I'm going to just enjoy it and see where the night takes us.

I let out a loud yawn. "I'll have to put my same clothes back on. I didn't pack a lot."

He turns on the shower and lets it hit his hand while he tests the temperature. When it's warm enough, he grabs me and helps me in. As soon as the hot spray hits my body, I groan. His breath is right next to my ear. "You don't need any clothes. I plan on keeping you naked the rest of the weekend."

I lean into him. "I like the sound of that."

He tips my chin up and searches my eyes. "We should probably talk about the fact that I didn't use a condom. I'm clean."

I gulp because I can't believe I didn't think about that. I've always been the responsible one. Heck, I have a brand-new box of condoms in my bag that I bought and brought with me, and I didn't even think to use them. He knows I'm clean. I wouldn't have been able to do the auction otherwise, so the only thing we have to worry about is pregnancy. I try to calculate in my head, but it's worthless. Right now, nothing is computing. "I didn't think—"

He shrugs and pulls me into his arms. "It's okay. I wouldn't have wanted to wear a condom anyway, Maggie. I don't want anything between us. All I want to feel is you."

I push the thought of pregnancy to the back of my brain. I know I should be worried, but I can't bring myself to be right now. Nope, all I can think about is how good it feels to be wrapped in his arms.

I lean my head against his chest. "You think I can sleep with you tonight, Ben?"

He rests his chin on the top of my head. "In my arms, in my bed is where I want you, Maggie."

I let out a satisfied sigh as he puts soap on his hands and starts to clean me. A girl could get used to this.

BEN

There's no way I can let her go.

The weekend is over, and tomorrow she plans to leave here and go to work. She has some kind of event tomorrow night for the mayor, and all I can think is the fact that I can't let her go. I don't want to.

"Do you like your job?"

She looks up at me with a smile. "You mean do I like working for you at Moonshine Distilleries?"

I bite my lip and wait for her to continue. She rolls her eyes. "Yeah, I love my job."

A part of me is glad to know she likes her job, but the other side, the one that is possessive and going fucking crazy at the thought of her walking away from me, is overwhelmed.

She points at me across the couch. "What's that frown about?"

I'm sitting on the opposite end of the couch with her feet in my lap. I want to slide down and pull her against me, but I know if I'm going to have this conversation with her, I need to do it with a little bit of distance between us. I ignore her question and ask my own. "So you like going into the office?"

Her eyes are glued to mine, and she shrugs. "I like going into the office. Elana said I could work from home whenever I wanted to. I'm fortunate that I can do my job from anywhere, but it was weird for me when I tried to work from home. It was lonely."

I massage her calves, and she moans. "That feels good."

I go deeper, working her muscles. "What if you worked a few days from home?"

She sits up and pulls her legs from my grip and sits cross-legged on the couch facing me. "Are you firing me, Ben?"

"What? No. Why would you think that? You do a phenomenal job. Sales are up since you took over social media. Hell no, I'm not firing you."

She tilts her head to the side and searches my eyes. "So what's with all this talk about working from home? You don't want me in the office?" She claps her hand to her head. "Oh my God, you don't want anyone to know about us." She looks at me with hurt in her eyes. "I'm not a blabbermouth. I won't tell anyone if that's how you want to keep it."

She gets up from the couch, but I grab her waist and pull her down onto my lap. She shimmies back and forth on my thighs, and my cock comes to life. I hold back my groan. "Stop moving or I'm going to bend you over this couch and fuck some sense into you, Maggie."

She stops moving, and I turn her around until she's straddling my lap. She's in one of my white T-shirts and her panties. The only thing stopping me from pulling my cock out and sliding into her is knowing that I know she needs a break and that I need to have this talk with her. "Look at me."

She looks at me, but the trust I've worked to build over the last day seems to have disappeared. "I'm looking at you."

I smile because she drives me crazy, but I wouldn't want it any other way. "Talk to me."

She juts her chin out. "Yeah, I can work from home if that's what I need to do."

I look to the open door where my office is. "I can put another desk in there."

She looks over to where I'm looking and then back

at me. Confusion is etched on her face. "What? You want me to work from here some days?"

I'm fucking this up. I put my hands on her hips and slide her farther down my legs until her panty-clad pussy is cradling my hard cock. "Let me start over. I want you to move in here with me. If you want to go into the office every day, that's fine. If you're willing to work from home a few days a week, I'll make it worth your while."

Her mouth falls open, and she closes it before opening it again. "Wait... uh, when you said home, you meant here?"

I nod. "Yeah, I want this to be your home. I want you here with me."

She bites her lower lip. "Are you sure about this?"

She still doesn't get it. Every thought I have is about her. There's nothing I wouldn't do to have her in my life permanently, even moving off this mountain if she wanted me to. "I love you, Maggie. I want us to be together. Wherever you're at, that's where I want to be."

She puts her hands on my chest. "So if I wanted to live on this mountain with you, that would make you happy?"

"Fuck yeah, I'd be happy, but you need to be happy

too. I wouldn't want you do anything unless it's something you really wanted."

She seems to consider that. "I would be happy here with you. But there's something you need to know before we go any further."

I nod without worry. There's nothing she could say that would change the way I feel about her. "Tell me."

Her hands slide down my chest, and she places them on her belly. "I figured out dates and all that. There's a likely chance I could be pregnant already."

She's looking at me worriedly, and I'm anxious to relieve her of any worry. "That's what I was hoping for. From the moment I laid eyes on you, I pictured you round with my baby. I hope you're pregnant, Maggie."

"You do?" she asks in amazement.

"Fuck, yeah, I do."

I tease the hem of her shirt, and she raises her arms as I pull it off.

I push my finger to the wet material at her pussy. "But just in case, maybe we should give it another go. I'm all for trying until we get it right."

"Yes," she moans as I work her clit through the sodden material.

I grab on to her panties and rip them right down

the middle. She gasps, and her eyes darken. My girl likes it when I take what I want. She puts her hand down the waistband of my shorts and pulls me out the top. With no hesitation, she gets into position and impales herself on my hard shaft. "Take me, Ben. Make me yours."

I cup the side of her neck, forcing her eyes to mine. "You are mine. You've always been mine."

"Yes," she groans as I lift my hips up to meet her.

Over and over, I thrust into her while telling her she's mine.

EPILOGUE
MAGGIE

One Year Later

"Can I buy you a drink?"

I look over at the man that is my husband's complete opposite. He has a Rolex around his wrist. His hair is neat and tidy, and he's clean-shaven. "I don't drink, and the drinks are free."

"Come on. You can't expect me to drink alone."

I move back from the table and stand up, my hand on my belly that looks as if I'm going to pop at any minute. The man's eyes are huge, and I'm thinking it's because he had no clue I was pregnant, but I realize quickly what has him spooked. My husband's hand snakes around my body and cups my belly. He pulls me against him, and I look up, seeing the glare on his face. The other man doesn't stand a chance. Ben is pretty laid back about most things, but in the past year, I've found that he is very possessive of me.

I turn in his arms, knowing he's jealous. The only thing that calms him down is when I go to my tiptoes, whisper, "Hey, husband," and press my lips to his.

And just like that, we both forget about everyone else.

The kiss is not considered appropriate when we're standing in the middle of the fundraiser for his family's company, but neither one of us seem to care. Even a year later, we can't get enough of each other.

I only pull back when I feel his bulge pressing into my belly. "You okay?"

His jaw is pulled tight. "I'm going to make this speech, and then I'm taking you home."

I lift my shoulders in a shrug. "You won't get any complaints out of me."

He leans down to whisper in my ear, "Only because you know I can't stand it when another man flirts with you. I'll fuck you until you don't think about anything except for me and how good I make you feel."

I fan my face, feeling the scorching heat of his words. When he's jealous, he's insatiable. I know that

I'm guaranteed at least three orgasms when I get home. I shove him away from me. "Go give your speech. Edward and Elana are glad you're doing it. But make it fast. I'm ready to go home."

He kisses me again, and I watch as my big, strapping mountain man makes his way to the stage. He shakes hands with his brother as he gets to the microphone. Elana comes to stand next to me and holds my hand. "Thank you," she whispers.

"What for?" I ask her, without taking my eyes off her brother.

She leans her head on my shoulder, and we listen to Ben talk about his parents, his brother and sister, and the family business. "You gave me my brother back."

Her words are simple but heartfelt. The change in Ben this past year has been amazing to see up close and personal. He's happy, that much is obvious, and he spends every day of his life making sure I am too.

I squeeze her hand and tune into what Ben is saying. "And I want to thank my wife, Maggie. She planned all this and makes sure it all goes off without a hitch. She's an amazing woman that brings out the best in all of us. I love you, Maggie."

I wipe at a tear and smile proudly up at him. He closes his speech, and as he comes off the stage, several people try and stop him, but he's a man on a mission. He makes his way to me and his sister. He hugs Elana and then turns to me. I know that look in his eye, and I go to him as he wraps his hand around mine. "Ready?"

He is pulling me toward the door. "With you, I'm always ready."

Impatiently, he leans down and picks me up in his arms. I laugh and pat him on the chest. "Ben, put me down. I'm too big to be carrying."

He strides out of the building. "You're perfect, Maggie. And you're mine."

I lean my head against his chest and agree. "I'm yours."

We may have had a rocky start, but I wouldn't change a thing. I don't tell many people the story about how I was auctioned to the mountain man, but I sure am glad I was.

HIGHEST BIDDER
SERIES

The series where the Highest Bidder always wins.

Welcome to a one-of-a-kind Auction House where humans, shifters, and aliens bid on love.

These ultra-rich men are ready to bring home their virgin prizes.

Are you ready to join in and wish you were the one on the auction block?

Nine standalone stories by best-selling steamy romance authors, Hope Ford, Olivia T. Turner, and Michele Mills. You've never seen an auction house like this!

Get the series here: Highest Bidder

Auctioned to the Alien Beast by Michele Mills

Auctioned to the Grizzly Shifter by Olivia T. Turner

Auctioned to the Lumberjack by Hope Ford

Auctioned to the Pack Alpha by Olivia T. Turner

Auctioned to the Cowboy by Hope Ford

Auctioned to the Tusk Warrior by Michele Mills

Auctioned to the Mountain Man by Hope Ford

Auctioned to the Kodiak Shifter by Olivia T. Turner

Auctioned to the Alien Boss by Michele Mills

Whiskey Run Series

Want more of Whiskey Run?

Whiskey Run

Faithful - He's the hot, say-it-like-it-is cowboy, and he won't stop until he gets the woman he wants.

Captivated - She's a beautiful woman on the run... and I'm going to be the one to keep her.

Obsessed - She's loved him since high school and now he's back.

Seduced - He's a football player that falls in love with the small town girl.

Devoted - She's a plus size model and he's a small town mechanic.

Whiskey Run: Savage Ink

Virile - He won't let her go until he puts his mark on her.

Torrid - He'll do anything to give her what she wants.

Rigid - If you love reading about emotionally wounded men and the women that help them overcome their past, then you'll love Dawson and Emily's story.

Whiskey Run: Cowboys Love Curves

Obsessed Cowboy - She's the preacher's daughter and she's

off limits.

Whiskey Run: Heroes

Ransom - He's on a mission he can't lose.

Redeem - He's in love with his sister's best friend.

Submit - She's his fake wife but he wants to make it real.

Forbid - They have a secret romance but he's about to stake his claim.

Whiskey Run: Sugar

One Night Love - Her one night stand wants more.

Rebound Love - She's falling for the rebound guy.

Second Chance Love - He is not a man to ignore... especially when he asks for a second chance.

Bad Boy Love - He's a bad boy that wants her good.

Whiskey Run: Guardians MC

Protective Biker - She needs his protection and he'll give it to her. But he's going to need her heart in exchange.

Broken Biker - There's only one woman for him...

Relentless Biker - He won't stop until he has her back.

FREE BOOKS

JOIN ME!

JOIN MY NEWSLETTER & READERS GROUP

www.AuthorHopeFord.com/Subscribe

JOIN MY READERS GROUP ON FACEBOOK

www.FB.com/groups/hopeford

Find Hope Ford at www.authorhopeford.com

About the Author

USA Today Bestselling Author Hope Ford writes short, steamy, sweet romances. She loves tattooed, alpha men, instant love stories, and ALWAYS happily ever afters. She has over 100 books and they are all available on Amazon.

To find me on Pinterest, Instagram, Facebook, Goodreads, and more:

www.AuthorHopeFord.com/follow-me

Printed in Great Britain
by Amazon

25952450R00067